What Is an Insect?

Susan Canizares • Mary Reid

Scholastic Inc.
New York • Toronto • London • Auckland • Sydney

Acknowledgments

Science Consultants: Patrick R. Thomas, Ph.D., Bronx Zoo/Wildlife Conservation Park; Glenn Phillips, The New York Botanical Garden; **Literacy Specialist:** Maria Utefsky, Reading Recovery Coordinator, District 2, New York City

Design: MKR Design, Inc.

Photo Research: Barbara Scott

Endnotes: Susan Russell

Photographs: Cover: (bl) C.A. Henley, (tr) Robert & Linda Mitchell; p.1: (tl) Robert & Linda Mitchell, (tr) Barbara Gerlach/DRK Photo, (bl) J.H. Robinson/Photo Researchers, Inc. (br) Robert & Linda Mitchell; p. 2, 3 & 4: Robert & Linda Mitchell; p.5: Photo Researchers, Inc.; p. 6: Barbara Gerlach/DRK Photo; p. 7: S. J. Krasemann/Peter Arnold, Inc.; p. 8: Robert & Linda Mitchell; p. 9: Larry Miller/Photo Researchers, Inc.; p. 10: J.H. Robinson/Photo Researchers, Inc.; p. 11: C.A. Henley; p. 12: (tl) C.A. Henley, (tr) Larry Miller/Photo Researchers, Inc., (bl) & (br) Robert & Linda Mitchell.

Library of Congress Cataloging-in-Publication Data
Canizares, Susan, 1960-
What is an insect? / Susan Canizares, Mary Reid.
p. cm. -- (Science emergent readers)
"Scholastic early childhood."--P. [4] of cover.
Includes index.
Summary: Uses photographs and simple text to explain the definition of an insect.
ISBN 0-590-39790-7 (pbk.: alk.paper)
1. Insects--Juvenile literature. [1. Insects.]
I. Reid, Mary. II. Title. III. Series.
QL467.2.C355 1998
595.7--dc21 97-29203
CIP AC

10 03 02 01 00 99

What is an insect?

This is an insect.

This is not.

This is an insect.

This is not.

This is an insect.

This is not.

This is an insect.

This is not.

An insect has three body parts.

An insect has six legs.

Is it an insect?

What Is an Insect?

Insects are the most successful and numerous creatures on earth. There are more than 750,000 species of insect and most fit into four main groups:1) beetles; 2) butterflies and moths; 3) wasps, bees, and ants; 4) flies, gnats, and mosquitos. Insects have other special characteristics that can help you identify them. Here are a few to help you get started.

The Green Bottle Fly (left) is an insect. Wings are one of its characteristics. When it flies, it can carry diseases to people. The Malayan Green Frog (right) is not an insect, having only four legs and no wings!

The Honeybee (left) is one of man's insect helpers. It uses its wings and legs to bring pollen from one plant to another so that their life cycles can be completed. The Earthworm (right) has no legs at all and is not an insect.

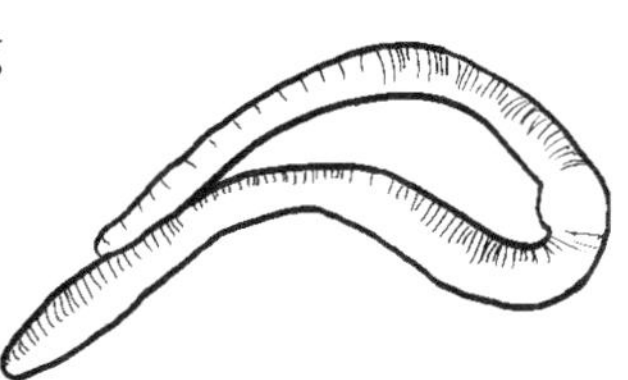

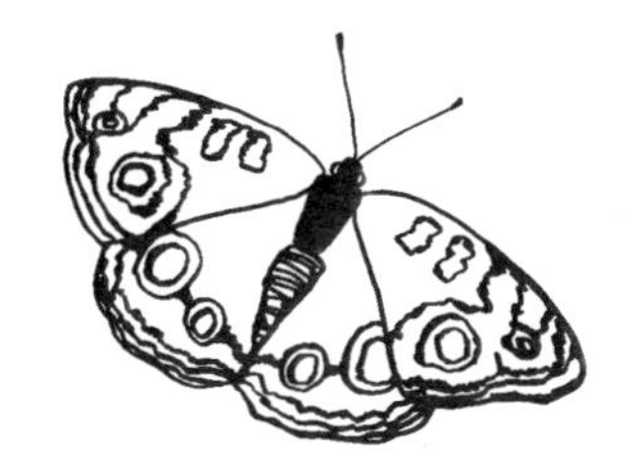

The Buckeye Butterfly (left) is part of the insect family. It has antennae and wings. Butterflies like the daylight, while their cousins, the moths, prefer the night. The eyes of the Ghost Crab (right) sit high on stalks that resemble antennae, but are not.

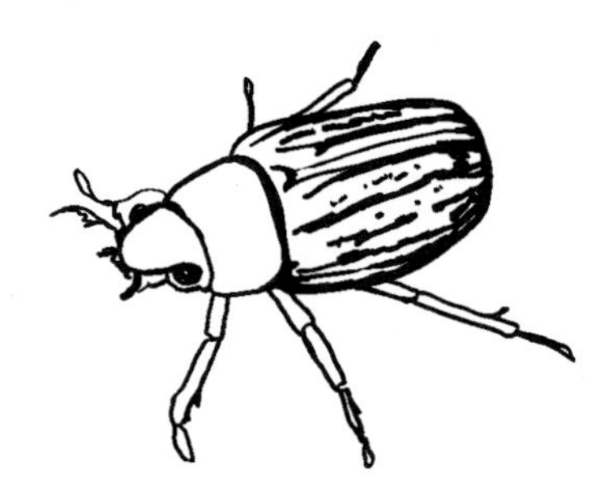

Beetles are known by the tough, armorlike wings that cover the back wings they use for flying. The Green Scarab Beetle (left) has just the right number of legs to identify it as an insect: six. The Centipede (right) has many legs and is not an insect.

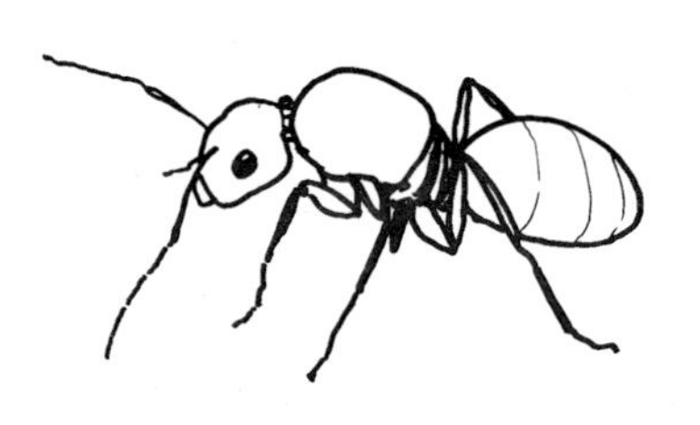

The Carpenter Ant (left) demonstrates the insect's three body parts: 1) the head, which usually has antennae; 2) the thorax, where the legs and wings are attached, has many muscles; 3) the abdomen holds all the organs needed for digestion, reproduction, and breathing. The Eucalyptus Tip Bug (right) demonstrates the six legs that all insects have.

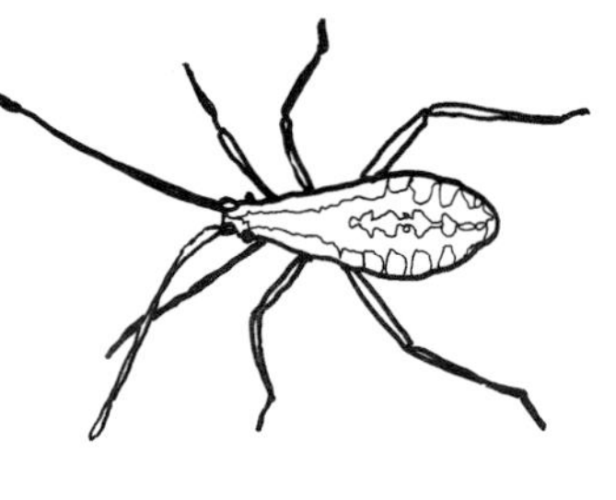

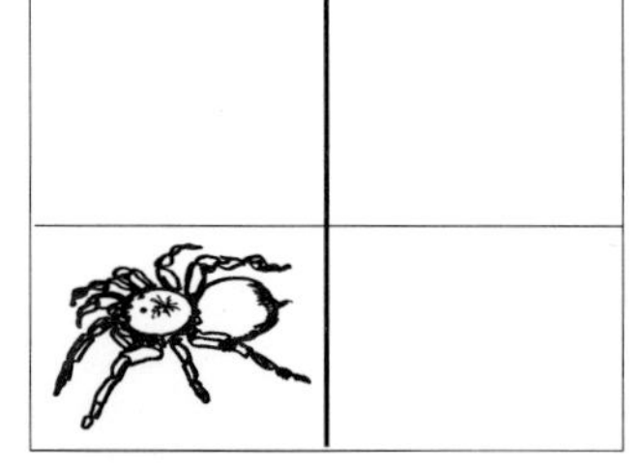

The Velvet-Bodied Tarantula (left) is the only new creature on the last page and is not an insect because it has only two body parts and eight legs. It is a member of the spider family.